Eagen, Rachel, 1979-
Cutting and self-injury
/
c2011.
33305227389?4
gi   0/14/11

W

P9-BJK-677

Straight Talk About...

CUTTING and SELF-INJURY

Rachel
Eagen

Crabtree Publishing Company
www.crabtreebooks.com

Straight
Talk About...

Developed and produced by: Plan B Book Packagers

Editorial director: Ellen Rodger

Art director: Rosie Gowsell-Pattison

Fictional Introductions: Rachel Eagen

Editor: Molly Aloian

Project coordinator: Kathy Middleton

Production coordinator: Margaret Amy Salter

Prepress technician: Margaret Amy Salter

Consultant: Susan Rodger, PhD., C. Psych.,
Psychologist and Professor Faculty of Education,
The University of Western Ontario

Special thanks to: Lisa M.

Photographs:
Title page: iStockPhoto.com; p. 4: Andrija Kovac/
Shutterstock Inc.; p. 6: Mikael Damkier/Shutterstock
Inc.; p. 8: Muellek Josef/Shutterstock Inc.; p. 9: Lucas
Allen White/Shutterstock Inc.; p. 10: iStockPhoto.com;
p. 11: Catmando/Shutterstock Inc.; p. 12: Peter Close/
Shutterstock Inc.; p. 14: (left) iStockPhoto.com,
(right) Svetlana Amelina/Shutterstock Inc.; p. 15:
iStockPhoto.com; p. 16: Psycho/Shutterstock Inc.; p. 17:
Veter67/Shutterstock Inc.; p. 18: iStockPhoto.com; p. 19:
s26/Shutterstock Inc.; p. 20: Netfalls/Shutterstock Inc.;
p. 22: Kameel4u/Shutterstock Inc.; p. 24: Monkey
Business Images/Shutterstock Inc.; p. 26: Epic Stock/
Shutterstock Inc.; p. 27: Anyka/Shutterstock Inc.;
p. 28: Berislav Kovacevic/Shutterstock Inc.; p. 29:
iStockPhoto.com; p. 30: Viviamo/Shutterstock Inc.;
p. 32: Ansar80/Shutterstock Inc.; p. 33: Studio Foxy/
Shutterstock Inc.; p. 34: iStockPhoto.com; p. 35:
ImageryMajestic/Shutterstock Inc.; p. 36:
iStockPhoto.com; p. 37: SRNR/Shutterstock Inc.;
p. 38: (right) iStockPhoto.com; (left) Blazej Maksym/
Shutterstock Inc.; p. 40: Andrzej80/Shutterstock Inc.;
p. 42: Yuliyan Velchev/Shutterstock Inc.

Library and Archives Canada Cataloguing in Publication

Eagen, Rachel, 1979-
    Cutting and self-injury / Rachel Eagen.

(Straight talk about--)
Includes index.
Issued also in an electronic format.
ISBN 978-0-7787-2130-7 (bound).--ISBN 978-0-7787-2137-6 (pbk.)

    1. Cutting (Self-mutilation)--Juvenile literature.
2. Self-mutilation--Juvenile literature. I. Title.
II. Series: Straight talk about-- (St. Catharines, Ont.)

RJ506.S44E23 2010   j616.85'82   C2010-902767-1

Library of Congress Cataloging-in-Publication Data

Eagen, Rachel.
    Cutting and self-injury / Rachel Eagen.
        p. cm. -- (Straight talk about)
    Includes index.
    ISBN 978-0-7787-2137-6 (pbk. : alk. paper) --
    ISBN 978-0-7787-2130-7 (reinforced library binding : alk. paper)
    -- ISBN 978-1-4271-9543-2 (electronic (pdf))
    1. Cutting (Self-mutilation)--Juvenile literature. 2. Self-
mutilation in adolescence--Juvenile literature. I. Title. II. Series.

    RJ506.S44E24 2011
    616.85'8200835--dc22

                                                    2010016398

Crabtree Publishing Company

www.crabtreebooks.com   1-800-387-7650

Printed in China/082010/AP20100512

Copyright © **2011 CRABTREE PUBLISHING COMPANY.** All rights reserved. No part of this publication may be reproduced,
stored in a retrieval system or be transmitted in any form or by any means, electronic, mechanical, photocopying, recording, or otherwise,
without the prior written permission of Crabtree Publishing Company. In Canada: We acknowledge the financial support of the Government
of Canada through the Book Publishing Industry Development Program (BPIDP) for our publishing activities.

Published in Canada
Crabtree Publishing
616 Welland Ave.
St. Catharines, ON
L2M 5V6

Published in the United States
Crabtree Publishing
PMB 59051
350 Fifth Avenue, 59th Floor
New York, NY 10118

Published in the United Kingdom
Crabtree Publishing
Maritime House
Basin Road North, Hove
BN41 1WR

Published in Australia
Crabtree Publishing
386 Mt. Alexander Rd.
Ascot Vale (Melbourne)
VIC 3032

CONTENTS

Heather shut the door to her room. Her heart was racing. She could hear the blood roaring in her head. She felt like she was going to explode.

They were screaming at each other again. They hadn't even noticed her come in. She had walked straight past them, like a ghost. These were her parents. And she was the invisible daughter.

She couldn't breathe. Where was her sewing kit? The closet. Her hiding place. She locked the door to her room and went to the closet. She took the sewing kit down from the top shelf. Her hands were shaking. She opened the kit. Just the sight of the little scissors and rows of needles made her feel better.

She shut the closet door and crouched down on the floor. Her breathing was still ragged. She took the sharp little scissors and pulled up her sleeve. The cuts on the inside of her arm were starting to heal. The black little scabs were hard and ugly. She pressed the scissors to her arm and pushed them into her skin. I'm here, she thought. I'm real. She pushed harder until she felt the familiar pain, sharp at first, then smoothing out. She closed her eyes. Finally, she could breathe.

Introduction
Hurting on Purpose

Heather is struggling with a lot of overwhelming feelings. The fighting between her parents is only one of her problems. How she's dealing with it is another. Self-injury is the act of hurting your body on purpose. You might be able to guess that it isn't a healthy way of dealing with things. But like Heather, you might not know that people who self-injure need help to stop.

In this book, you will learn more about self-injury, including why people do it and why it is dangerous. You will also learn healthier ways to cope, where you can get help, and how to reach out to a friend.

"People always tell me to think positively and things will feel better, but how can I think positive when my mind is numb? I can't think at all about anything. Everything is all just too much."
Natalie, aged 14.

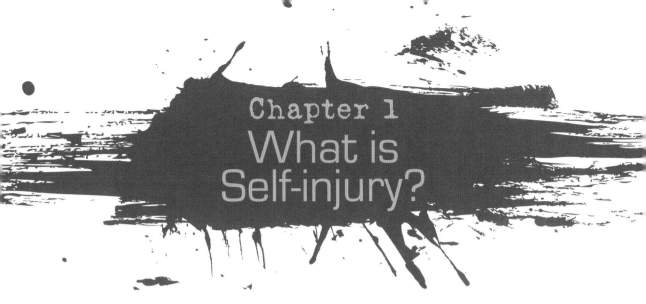

Chapter 1
What is Self-injury?

Self-injury is the act of deliberate hurting of your own body. It is usually repetitive—people who self-injure do it regularly, sometimes at the same time of day. **Psychologists** describe self-injury as a **coping mechanism**. It is the way some people deal with really intense emotions. For some, self-injury spirals out of control very quickly.

Is This Self-injury?

People self-injure in many different ways. The most common type of self-injury is called cutting. It involves using a sharp object, such as a knife, razor blade, scissors, or glass, to make cuts in the skin. The cuts are deep enough to bleed, but they are not usually so deep that medical attention is needed. The biggest risk of hurting yourself this way is infection. Other ways that people self-injure are by placing hot objects against their skin to burn it, picking at scabs repeatedly, and inserting sharp objects, such as needles or splinters of wood, under the skin. Pulling out clumps of your own hair is another form of self-injury known as trichotillomania. Hitting or slapping yourself is another way to self-injure, as well as drinking poisonous chemicals.

Where Are the Wounds?

Self-injury is often done to places that are hard to spot, such as the inside of the arms, the thighs, and belly. Sometimes, people self-injure in more obvious places, such as the wrists and face. It is common for people to hide their wounds under clothing, such as long sleeves and pants, as well as hats or scarves. Self-injury is a very secretive act, which is why it can go on for a long time without anyone else knowing about it.

Other Ways of Hurting Yourself

Inflicting wounds is the most common type of self-injury, but people hurt themselves in many other ways. Using drugs and drinking large amounts of alcohol are two commonly recognized ways to harm your body. These behaviors can be just as destructive and just as **addictive** as cutting. Some doctors believe that smoking or binging on junk food are forms of self-injury. These are behaviors people use to deal with stress. In fact, any type of behavior that harms you, either physically or emotionally, can be considered self-injurious.

Some doctors think that excessive tattooing and body piercing can be a form of self-injury.

Who Self-injures?

There are a lot of conflicting numbers out there about how many people in the world self-injure. There are two reasons for this. It is rare for a person who self-injures to admit to it, unless they are getting **treatment** for it. Secondly, the definition of self-injury has only recently been expanded to include behaviors such as drug and alcohol abuse.

In the United States, studies report that around 20 percent of high school students have admitted to some form of self-injurious behavior. Many researchers have said that self-injury is more common among girls. Self-injury usually starts in adolescence, around the age of 14. However, self-injury is not limited to teenagers, as some children and adults also self-injure. Something that all people that self-injure have in common is low **self-esteem**.

Experts say the outside wounds of self-injury are a reflection of the inside wounds.

A Silent Cry

Self-injury is a very private act. It is almost always something that people do alone, and it is not something that people want to talk about unless they are ready to get help.

Some people who self-injure express fear and anxiety about others finding out. Most adolescents are terrified that their parents will discover that they are self-injuring. Something else that is common among people who self-injure is the feeling that the wounds give a voice to the pain they feel inside. The scabs and scars somehow represent feelings that people do not know how to express in other ways. It is a way of letting those emotions out. This is partly why people do it.

A Coping Mechanism

Self-injury can be very difficult to understand, both for the people who do it and the people who care about them. There can be many reasons why someone self-injures, but not everyone who self-injures can explain why they do it. Psychologists think of self-injury as a coping mechanism. It is a way of dealing with very upsetting emotions or life situations. It is a way of gaining a sense of control when life feels **chaotic**. For some people, self-injury is a way to feel less numb, or to really feel something, even if that feeling is pain.

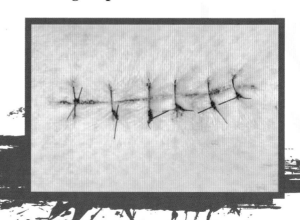

Feeling Worse, Not Better

Self-injury is not a healthy coping mechanism. In fact, self-injury just makes your problems worse. It only works in the moment. Self-injury provides a temporary sense of relief, but you might feel other negative emotions, such as guilt, sadness, and depression, just moments after self-injuring. It is also important to remember that self-injury is not a solution—it does not make any other problems go away. It is a short-term escape.

The Tip of the Iceberg

Self-injury involves hurting yourself, but the people who do it are already hurting. There is always something else going on in the person's life that is making them feel overwhelmed and out of control. Some people who self-injure have suffered at the hands of an abuser, while others are struggling with huge changes in their lives, such as a breakup, the divorce of parents, or a move to another country. Self-injury is often paired with other types of problems, such as **depression, anxiety,** eating disorders, and other mental health issues.

"It's okay to have strong feelings. It's also okay to talk about them. It is hard to cope with things on your own."
-Rebeccah, counselor.

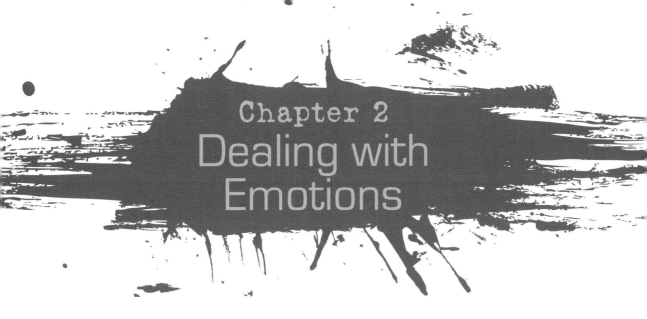

Chapter 2
Dealing with Emotions

It can be very hard to understand why people self-injure. Everyone is different, so there are no hard and fast rules for why people do it. The important thing to remember is that self-injury serves a purpose in the moment.

Relief

Okay, so self-injury is a coping mechanism. But how does it help people cope? Many people who self-injure say that the pain gives them relief from other upsetting feelings. Inflicting pain provides an emotional rush, similar to the feeling you might get from sprinting down the road or riding a roller coaster. That release of feeling is a break from the bad feelings they are struggling with. This is part of why self-injury can become addictive. Just like you might want to ride the same roller coaster again and again, someone who self-injures might be driven to cut themselves over and over, just to experience the short rush of positive feelings they feel after hurting themselves.

Distraction

Another reason why people self-injure is that it gives them something else to think about. It is a way of focusing their attention on something other than what is bothering them. This works in two ways. First, the act of **inflicting** pain has a way of focusing the mind. The painful sensations block out what else is happening in a person's mind. Second, the sight of the wound provides something else for the person to focus on. The appearance of blood grabs their attention and keeps their mind from wandering back into the problems they are facing.

"The first time I cut, I was 14, after two close family members died within a year of each other. It gave me relief. I felt like I was releasing pent up frustration and I would feel calm afterward."
Sasha, aged 17.

Voicing the Pain

Many people who self-injure say that they cannot find other ways to express their feelings. They feel completely overwhelmed by emotions such as anger, frustration, fear, sadness, and other feelings, but they do not know how to express these emotions in healthy ways. Some people might call a friend, go for a run, or punch a pillow when they feel overwhelmed. People who self-injure express their emotions by hurting themselves. Self-injury declares the intensity of their pain when words and other actions cannot.

Emotions can be tough to deal with, especially for people who don't feel comfortable talking about personal issues.

Gaining Control

Self-injury is sometimes a means for people to feel in control of what is happening in their lives. People who self-injure feel overwhelmed not only by their feelings, but by experiences that they cannot control. For example, a bad breakup, the divorce of parents, an incurable illness, physical disability, failing school, being bullied, and other traumatic experiences can make people feel helpless.

Not knowing how to deal with stress can make people panic.

Self-injuring is something that a person decides to do when they feel upset. They are responsible for causing the wounds, and that helps them to feel that they can control at least this one thing when everything around them feels chaotic.

Becoming Real

Many people who self-injure say that their emotions only feel real after they have self-injured. This is especially true for people who struggle to explain what they feel. They might use words like "bad" or "awful" to describe their feelings, but not words like "depressed," "angry," or "sad." Sometimes, their feelings are so jumbled that they are totally lost in them. They become frustrated by not being able to put a label on their feelings.

Disconnected and in Pain

Many people who self-injure have gone through painful experiences. The pain of these experiences has a way of making people feel that they deserve to suffer. They might start to feel that they are unworthy of happiness. In this way, self-injury is a way of punishing themselves when they feel that they deserve to feel bad.

When people have suffered from a traumatic experience, it is also common for them to feel **dissociated**, or disconnected from their bodies or the world around them. Dissociation is difficult to understand if you have never experienced it before. Basically, it feels a bit like floating through space. People who experience dissociation say that they feel very detached, or separate, from their bodies. They feel as though nothing that happens to them is really happening. They cannot feel where their bodies start and end.

Dissociation can help people who have experienced something horrible, by helping them feel removed from the trauma they have experienced. But over time, dissociation can become **automatic**. In other words, sometimes people cannot control when they slip into daydream mode and when they are fully awake. Self-injury is a way some people cope with dissociation. Cutting helps people to feel that they are inside their own skin, that they exist, and that their bodies are real.

"When I was cutting, I was punishing myself. Once I took the punishment, I was able to move on."
-Michelle, aged 17, in recovery.

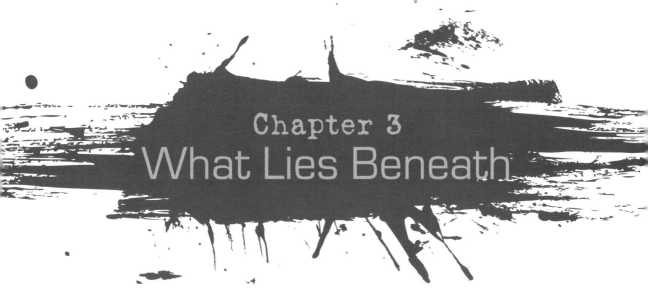

Chapter 3
What Lies Beneath

Self-injury temporarily helps people feel better, or in control, and provides them relief from disturbing or upsetting emotions. For some people, it is also a way to communicate their feelings. But are there reasons for what leads people to cope this way in the first place?

Deeper than Skin

As you might have guessed, self-injury is not just about dealing with problems. Usually, self-injury is a symptom of a larger, deeper problem. For the most part, self-injury is a warning sign that there is a **disorder** at play. In other words, the disorder is what leads a person to want to self-injure. The disorder often exists long before the desire to self-injure occurs. For this reason, **recovery** usually means addressing, or dealing with, the disorder, as well as finding healthier ways to cope with and express the feelings surrounding it.

Some people are surprised to learn self-injury is more than skin deep.

So What Is a Disorder?

A mental disorder is a broad term that describes any kind of behavior or way of thinking that is thought to be different from "normal" behaviors and ways of thinking. Normal can be hard to define, but there are general ranges in human behavior that are thought to be healthy. When a person has a disorder, they think or act differently than people who are considered to be healthy. These differences can be subtle, or hardly noticeable, as well as obvious, or very noticeable. There are thousands of mental disorders known to mental health professionals today. Several of them relate to self-injury.

Self-injury can hide, or mask, other disorders.

What Are Obsessive Behaviors?

You have probably heard the word "obsession" before. Basically, an obsession is a **recurring** thought that makes it difficult to think about anything else. People who are really interested in a particular sport might be described as being "obsessed." In mental health, an obsession means more than that. Obsessive behaviors are ways that people act to satisfy recurring thoughts, or obsessions. These behaviors interfere with their lives. Self-injury is an obsessive behavior. The thought of cutting, burning, or self-injuring in other ways becomes so powerful in a person's mind that it is almost impossible for them to avoid doing it.

Depression

Depression is a disorder that involves feelings of sadness and worthlessness. People who are depressed often have difficulty concentrating, sleeping, and eating. They suffer with these feelings nonstop for at least two weeks, but often much longer. There can be different reasons for depression. For some, an upsetting experience or a brutal disappointment can throw them into a pit of depression. Other people are just more prone to feeling that way from time to time because of the way their brains work.

Someone who is depressed might turn to self-injury as a way of dealing with their feelings of sadness and worthlessness. Depression is a curable disorder that can be treated in positive, healthy ways. Self-injury does not help people treat their depression. In fact, self-injuring only makes the depression worse.

Anxiety

Another disorder that is linked to self-injury is anxiety. You might feel anxious from time to time, such as before you take a big test or give a presentation at school. Anxiety is a normal, healthy response to stress, but anxiety disorders prevent people from living normal lives. Anxiety disorders can sometimes cause people to have panic attacks, in which they become totally paralyzed by their anxiety. The feelings of helplessness that people with anxiety disorders often experience can lead them to self-injure. Self-injury can make them feel more in control.

Abuse and PTSD

Post-traumatic stress disorder (PTSD) can can be triggered by a traumatic experience that threatens a person's safety. A lot of people who have lived through war, physical, emotional, or sexual abuse, and other traumas, suffer from PTSD. It is common for people who suffer from PTSD to relive the memory of what happened to them over and over again. This can be very upsetting. For some people, self-injury is a way to escape these frightening feelings. It is also a way to distract their minds from haunting memories.

Eating Disorders and Self-injury

Eating disorders are eating behaviors that are not considered normal. Studies have revealed that around 45 percent of people who suffer from eating disorders, such as anorexia nervosa and bulimia, also self-injure in some way.

People who suffer from eating disorders experience a lot of the feelings that are linked to self-injury. Most importantly, people who have eating disorders are often unable to control or deal with their emotions, which is common among people who self-injure.

Eating disorders and self-injury are sometimes linked.

22

Myths about Self-injury

There are many beliefs about self-injury, but not all of them are true. Here are some of the common misunderstandings about self-injury:

Myth: Self-injury is just a way to get attention.

Fact: Self-injury is usually hidden. People who do it do not want others to know about it. Self-injury is a sign that there are some very serious problems happening in someone's life, and they need help and support.

Myth: Self-injury is contagious.

Fact: Having a friend or family member that self-injures does not put you at a higher risk for self-injuring. Friends or family members of people who self-injure might "try it out" to see how it feels, but it is not a habit that will stick unless there are other issues going on.

Myth: Only crazy people self-injure.

Fact: Self-injury is a sign that something is wrong in a person's life. In many cases, self-injury is a symptom of a mental health issue, such as an eating disorder or depression, but that does not mean that the person who is self-injuring is crazy or cannot be helped. People that self-injure are dealing with their problems the only way they know how.

Myth: Self-injury is easy to stop.

Fact: People who self-injure can stop, but it is very difficult to stop on their own. It takes time to replace bad coping mechanisms with good ones. Usually, help from a counselor or therapist is necessary. Support from family and friends is also important.

"It was always easier to accept blame rather than try to confront the real problem. It felt like everything was my fault, whether it was or not. So then I would cut to hurt myself or to feel the pain." Allie, aged 17.

Chapter 4
Healthy Behaviors

An urge is a powerful desire to do something, good or bad. It describes all of the feelings that occur before someone self-injures. People that self-injure often say they feel powerless against their urges. In other words, the urge to hurt themselves is so strong that they feel they cannot stop themselves from doing it. An important thing to know about urges is that they pass, no matter how strong they are.

Waiting It Out

If you can find a way to wait out urges, they become less powerful and you can move on. Here is an example: A craving for something sweet might give you the urge to walk down to the store to buy a candy bar. Sometimes, you can satisfy your craving by eating something else, like a spoonful of peanut butter. You might also try to busy yourself with an activity, like reading a book. In other words, you do not have to act on your urges. You can distract yourself by focusing on doing something else.

What are Triggers?

Triggers are the things that spark urges. Everyone who self-injures has different triggers. Usually, these triggers set off a chain reaction of negative feelings that lead them to self-injure. Some examples of triggers are failing a test at school, fighting with a friend or dating partner, and hearing your parents argue. What are your triggers? How do they make you behave? It is a good idea to write down your triggers. Knowing what they are is an important part of learning how to deal with them.

Making Choices

Try to think of urges as waves in an ocean. The waves build and rush toward shore, peaking before they crash on the sand. The urge to self-injure works in the same way. The feelings that come before you hurt yourself build until you feel completely powerless against them. But they are not more powerful than you. You can choose to stop self-injuring. It is not easy, but it is not impossible. You can choose healthier ways to deal with your feelings. When the urge strikes, find somewhere quiet and lie down. Take deep breaths while you wait for the waves to crash and die. Remember, this is not something that needs to control you.

Knowing your Feelings

One of the first steps in building healthy coping behaviors is naming your feelings. How do you feel before you self-injure? Do you feel sad, scared, depressed, angry, or helpless? What are some other words to describe how you feel before you self-injure? How do you feel after you self-injure? Do you feel calm, relieved, and safe? Do you experience anything else when you self-injure? For example, you might recall upsetting or happy memories before and after you self-injure.

You experience your feelings with your mind and body. The physical signs of an emotion are how we can tell what our feelings are. For example, the feeling of anxiety or panic might come with sweaty palms or a fluttery feeling in your stomach. Anger can make your heart beat faster or give you a headache. Paying attention to the way your body feels is another way you can identify your feelings.

It helps to be aware of what you are feeling. That means questioning your behavior in the moment.

Tracking your Feelings

Naming your feelings is a very important part of recovering from self-injury. Many people who self-injure feel that the pain they inflict on their bodies is the only way to voice what they feel. Putting other words to these feelings often lessens the need to express them through self-injuring.

It is also important to understand how you feel before and after you self-injure because it helps you identify what you are getting from self-injury. For example, if you feel unhappy or disappointed in yourself after you self-injure, then you might start to realize that self-injuring is not really helping you to feel any better.

Try exploring your feelings by writing them down before and after you self-injure. Do not worry if you do not know how to describe them. Your feelings are private and no one is going to judge the words you use. If it helps, try using colors instead of feelings. For example, black or red might help you describe feelings of anger. You also might describe anger as "loud." Do your thoughts feel very fast? Do you feel like screaming? Does your jaw feel tight? Is there a part of your body that hurts before you self-injure? Some people experience burning sensations in the body part that they cut. If this is how your body feels, write it down.

Getting Help

It can be very hard to stop self-injuring. It takes a lot of courage and strength. Many people need help to stop. They might need some form of **therapy**, such as counseling, medication, or another form of treatment. For many people, getting support from others is an important part of stopping self-injuring. That means telling people who might not know that you self-injure. Self-injury is often extremely private, and it is not something that many people want to share. But it is important to remember that the people who love you want you to be happy and safe in your life. The people who really care will not judge you for self-injuring, but will be there for you as you take those brave steps toward recovery.

Journal writing can help you understand or explain your feelings.

Negative Thinking

Write down the thoughts that often come to mind when you feel an urge to self-injure. When you are feeling calm, write down some positive things you can tell yourself when you start to think negatively.

Distractions

Make a list of things you can do that take a lot of focus or energy. Write down as many things as possible. For example, playing a challenging video game or going for a run. Distracting yourself from your urges to self-injure is a key to controlling them. People who self-injure often struggle with feelings of shame and guilt. Every time they cannot resist the urge to self-injure, they spiral into a dark hole of **regret** and shame.

Forgiveness

Forgiveness is a healthy behavior that helps you feel better about yourself. Think of the last time you apologized to someone. Forgiving yourself means that you do not expect to be perfect all of the time, in the same way that you do not expect others to be perfect.

Other Ways to Feel

Once you recognize an urge, and learn to describe the feelings that come with these urges, you can find better ways to express your feelings. For people that self-injure, this means that over time, they can replace self-injury with healthier coping mechanisms. You can also find ways to deal with stress so that your triggers are not as powerful as they once were.

Keep in mind that learning different ways to express your feelings is not about removing them. It is not about locking your feelings inside of you. It is about letting them out in ways that will not hurt you. There is nothing wrong with anger or anxiety, but there are good and bad ways to express these emotions. Here are some examples of healthy coping:

Calling a friend to talk about what's bothering you

Yelling into a pillow, or crying somewhere safe and private

Strenuous exercise, such as running or hitting a punching bag

Painting or drawing: what do your feelings look like?

Dancing to loud music or writing in a journal

Playing an instrument, such as the drums

It is important to take care of yourself when you are struggling with emotions and stress. This means getting enough sleep, eating healthy meals, and talking to someone you trust about your feelings.

"I've learned where my problems end and where other people's start. I refuse to accept responsibilty for other people's issues. Now that I am aware of that, I no longer have the need to hurt or punish myself."
Lisa M., adult survivor.

Chapter 5
Relating to Others

Getting support from others is very important for people who are trying to stop self-injuring. But since self-injury is such a private, personal act, many people are terrified of reaching out to others for help.

Will People Judge Me?

If you have kept your self-injuring a secret, it is natural to worry how people will react when you tell them. There is a chance that the people you share it with will react negatively. They might feel shocked, afraid, or even angry. They might have a lot of questions. People who have never self-injured might have a hard time understanding it. Some might need a bit of time with the news before they are able to support you. Others might not be able to handle it. Try to surround yourself with supportive people you can trust.

Why Do People Judge?

The idea of hurting your body can be really upsetting to some people. Hollywood movies paint a picture of how "cutters" look and behave. In these movies, characters that self-injure are attractive, white teenage girls who are spoiled and selfish. Usually, they do not seem to have any real problems. For this reason, people might believe that self-injury looks the same way in real life. People who self-injure can be any age, race, or **gender**. But some people might believe that those who self-injure are just bored or looking for attention. For recovery, you need help from people you can trust. Trust is not just about people judging you, for better or for worse. It is about being able to count on someone to help you.

Anybody Out There?

It is natural for people who self-injure to want to find others who are struggling with the same problem. Finding other people who self-injure can be both good and bad for your recovery. The bad part of making friends with others that self-injure is that it can be "triggering" to be around people who are at different stages of recovery than you.

Friends and family can be very supportive. Don't be afraid to ask them for help.

Online Support

Online **forums** are Web pages for people from all over the world to connect, share stories, and offer support. Users can post messages and receive answers from several other users. Support forums can be very helpful for people struggling with any kind of addiction, including self-injury. These forums allow users to be anonymous, which is great for people who have not yet told anyone else about their self-injuring. Self-injury blogs (online journals) offer the same kind of support.

There is a downside of digital, however. The information is often not moderated, especially in the case of blogs. That means that a professional counselor does not review the material to make sure it is accurate and that the advice being given is helpful and practical.

The other problem with online support communities is that it can make people who self-injure feel that there is no point in having "real" friends anymore. They might feel that their online friends are the only ones who understand what they are going through, and block out others in their lives who really care and want to offer support. In some cases, blogs and forums disguised as support communities defend self-injury as a normal, healthy behavior. Sometimes, these communities actually encourage people to self-injure.

Chapter 6
Seeking Help

When you begin to see self-injury as an unhealthy behavior, it is a sign that you are thinking of stopping. It is also a sign of wanting to learn healthier coping mechanisms. Congratulate yourself on coming this far.

Nothing to lose

Self-injury is an addictive behavior, which is why it can be really hard to stop. An activity that might help you is making a list of all of the ways in which self-injury is not helping you. One of these is that self-injury makes you feel badly about yourself. Self-injury also hurts your relationships with others. One of the most important things to remember about self-injury is that it does not make any of your problems go away. It just helps you forget about them for a while.

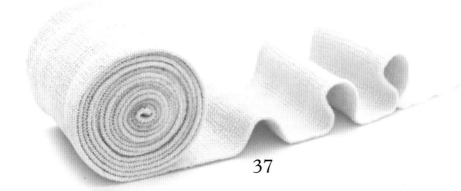

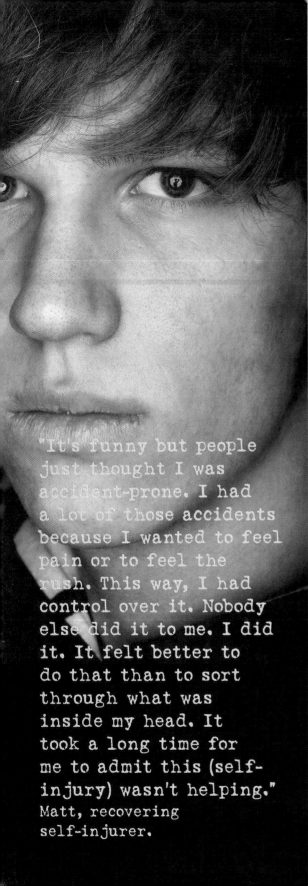

"It's funny but people just thought I was accident-prone. I had a lot of those accidents because I wanted to feel pain or to feel the rush. This way, I had control over it. Nobody else did it to me. I did it. It felt better to do that than to sort through what was inside my head. It took a long time for me to admit this (self-injury) wasn't helping."
Matt, recovering self-injurer.

Reaching Out

It is very hard to stop self-injuring on your own. You will probably need help from others. Try not to feel ashamed or guilty about needing help. Would you feel ashamed about asking for help opening the lid on a jar of pickles? Probably not. Try to think of your self-injury in the same way—as a problem that you need help with. Asking for help does not mean that the whole world has to know.

There is help out there. It takes a lot of courage to ask for it.

Who Can You Talk To?

Disclosure is a big word for something simple. It means telling someone something about yourself that is usually hard to talk about. Disclosure is an important part of recovery from self-injury because it allows other people to help and support you. It is not easy to disclose. You might feel worried about how people will react. Will they be angry with you? Will they judge you? Try to remember that the way people feel about your self-injury might change over time. Someone who is shocked to hear about it might just need some time before they can support you.

What to Say

It is natural to feel anxious about disclosing. Try to think of the good that can come from disclosing. You might feel relief about not having to hide it anymore. It might be useful to write down a few names of people who you trust. They can be parents, teachers, guidance counselors, neighbors, friends, and others. The list does not have to be long. Now think about what you want to say. Here are a few sentences that might help you: "I have something to tell you that is hard for me to talk about," or, "I need your help with something." It is a good idea to have this conversation in a safe, quiet place. Give yourself some time to get it off your chest. It will not take you long to say that you have been self-injuring and want to stop. But the person you tell might have questions for you. Try not to let this stop you from disclosing.

What Happens Next?

You did not start cutting one day. It happened over time. In the same way, it takes time to recover from self-injury. It might not get better right away. Depending on how people react to your news, things might even seem worse for a little while. You might have to tell more than one person to get the help that you need. The stress of talking about it might make your urges to self-injure even stronger at first. Hopefully, with the help of someone you trust, you will figure out a plan for stopping that works for you. The plan might involve visiting a doctor, getting counseling, or taking medication. Treatment also takes time.

Dealing with Slips

Most people cannot stop the moment they decide to. It is normal to "slip" once in a while. You might go for a few days or weeks without self-injuring, then suddenly start to self-injure

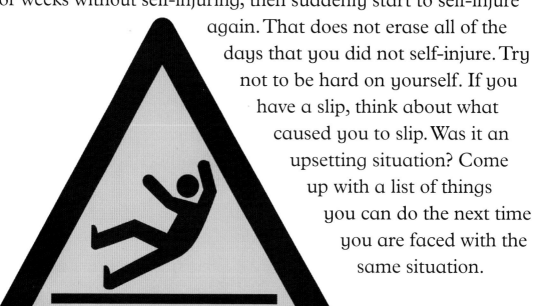

again. That does not erase all of the days that you did not self-injure. Try not to be hard on yourself. If you have a slip, think about what caused you to slip. Was it an upsetting situation? Come up with a list of things you can do the next time you are faced with the same situation.

For Friends and Family

It is natural to feel shocked, confused, and afraid when you learn that someone you care about has been self-injuring. You might feel hurt or sick to your stomach. Try to remember that it is very hard for someone who self-injures to open up about it. They may have struggled with what to say and who to tell for weeks or months. In a way, you can feel good about being the person they chose to tell. That must mean that they trust you. Do not betray that trust by sharing this information with others. Here are some other tips:

Try not to show that you are shocked, angry, or upset.

Listen. It is a healthy sign that this person is talking about their problem rather than hiding it away.

Use reassuring words, such as, "It's okay," "I'll help you," "We'll get through this together," and "I'm here for you."

Do not judge. Self-injury is not about being weak or sick. It is a symptom of a bigger problem.

Try to understand what is going on for this person. What other problems are at play? Self-injury can be a sign of abuse, so it is important to get at why this person is trying to cope in this way.

Find information on self-injury. Review the Web sites listed at the end of this book. Be aware that reading about self-injury might be upsetting for you, so do not force yourself.

Help the person find other support. Encourage them to see their doctor or help them find a counselor or psychologist. Go with them to visit the guidance counselor at school.

Chapter 7
Coping Toolbox

Every time you wait out an urge to self-injure, you have a reason to be proud of yourself. Urges lessen over time, which means that every time you stop yourself from self-injuring, you make the next urge less powerful. Having some tools for coping with urges is a very important part of recovery. Stopping self-injuring does not mean stopping the feelings that come with it. It means learning how to express your feelings in healthier ways. You might always feel urges to self-injure, but you can deal with those urges without hurting yourself.

Fifteen-minute Rule

How long did it take you to read this book? Chances are, it took longer than 15 minutes. Most psychologists agree that when the urge to self-injure strikes, it is important to keep busy for 15 minutes. If you can go 15 minutes without self-injuring, you have made it through the worst of the urge. Try to go for another 15 minutes. Repeat this as many times as it takes for the urge to pass.

Distraction and Coping Plan

In the moment, it can be very difficult to resist the urge to self-injure. It might help to make a list of things you can do to keep busy. The next time the urge strikes, look at your list and pick an activity. Here are some ideas:

Hold onto an ice cube; let it melt in your hand.

Wear a rubber band around your wrist (make sure it is not too tight). When you feel like self-injuring, snap the band.

Use a red marker to draw on the part of your skin that you usually hurt.

Eat something spicy.

Cut an onion and breathe in the smell until your eyes water.

Listen to loud music, take a bath, or go for a walk or run.

Do a favorite activity, such as playing video games or watching a movie.

Call a friend, play sports, or play with a pet.

Rip a sheet of paper into tiny pieces.

When you feel upset, it helps to focus on taking long, deep breaths. One way to do this is to find a safe, quiet place and lie down on your belly. Turn your face to one side and breathe deeply, in and out of your nose. Count to four as you inhale, count to four as you exhale. Do this for as long as it takes to feel better. Keep in touch with your feelings every day. It might help to write in a journal. Make a list of the things you like about yourself. Everyone has strengths, and so do you.

Q: Why do people think it's bad if I cut myself. I'm not hurting anyone?

A: Some people judge others who cut, because they cannot identify with the feelings and thoughts that make you want to cut. For the most part, people are not judging you, they are judging your behavior. The people who care about you want you to be safe, so if it seems like they are upset with you, it is probably just because they are worried about you. They might also wonder why you are doing this and what they can do to help.

Q: If I have to go to the hospital for cutting too deep, will a doctor be able to tell that I hurt myself?

A: It is hard to say if a doctor will be able to tell that you hurt yourself. It will depend on a lot of different things, such as how much time the doctor spends with you, whether the doctor has seen other people who self-injure in the past, and how much the doctor wants to get "involved" with your life. Something that might help you feel better is that a hospital or doctor's office is a good place for you to get help for self-injury. Doctors can put you in touch with helpful organizations that can give you the support you need to stop. They can also develop a treatment program that can help you replace self-injury with healthier coping mechanisms.

Q: When I disclose to someone like a teacher, will they report it to the police? Will they tell my parents?

A: It is hard to predict what someone will do after you disclose to them about your self-injury. If you are worried that they will tell someone else, you might want to start the conversation by saying, "I trust you with this information. I am not ready to tell anyone else yet, so please respect that." You cannot get into trouble with the police for self-injury.

Q: Cutting makes me feel better. How do I give it up?

A: It is not easy to give up cutting, but what you need to think about is whether or not cutting really helps you. For many people who cut, they feel just as badly about their lives just a few minutes after they cut. Replacing cutting with other behaviors gives you a chance to develop coping strategies that help you to build confidence, and keep you in a happy, healthy place.

Q: I stopped self-injuring a few times but I always start again. Is that normal?

A: It is very normal to experience "slips" when you decide to stop self-injuring. It can take a long time to stop wanting to self-injure. Try to forgive yourself for slips and go back to your list of replacement behaviors, such as those listed on page 43. You can also try some breathing exercises to try to calm down.

Q: Will my friends hate me if they find out I cut?

A: Your friends will not hate you if they find out about your self-injury. Some of them might struggle with the news, or show deep concern, but remember it is because they care about you. Friends who judge you are not the kind of friends who can offer you support.

Other Resources

There is a lot of information out there on self-injury and the types of people who self-injure. This kind of information can be very useful for people who are trying to stop self-injuring, or for friends and family members of people who self-injure. However, there is a lot of misinformation out there that gives people the wrong idea about what self-injury is, why people do it, and healthy ways to stop. Here are some trustworthy resources that can help you. The Web sites will contain useful information no matter which country you live in, but telephone numbers and referral services will be country-specific.

In the United States

Teen Health: Cutting
www.kidshealth.org/teen
Learn about cutting, from what it is to why people do it and how to reach out and help.

Help Guide: Self-injury
helpguide.org/mental/self_injury.htm
This site provides information for people who self-injure, as well as friends and parents. It also has good sections on how to stop and coping with stress.

S.A.F.E. Alternatives
www.selfinjury.com
Get tips on stopping self-injury and read support forums for others who are trying to recover.

The following hotlines can be used in the United States. If you are calling from another part of the world, feel free to call anyway as you can probably get a referral to another service in your region.

National Center for Victims of Crime
1-800-394-2255

National Mental Health Association
1-800-969-6642

Self-injury Hotline
1-800-DONT-CUT (1-800-366-8288)

In Canada
Deal.org: Self-injury
www.deal.org
Read up on what can lead someone to self-injure, the signs that someone you care about might be self-injuring, and find links to other helpful resources.

Mind Your Mind
www.mindyourmind.ca
Read up on mental health, get tips for coping with stress, play games, and take quizzes. You can also read stories from teens struggling to get by.

Kids Help Phone
www.kidshelpphone.ca
1-800-668-6868
Support forums for teens will help you see that you are not alone. Anonymous, confidential counseling is also available online. Phone counseling is available only to callers in Canada.

Glossary

addictive Something that is habit-forming and very hard to quit

anxiety A feeling of worry or unease; also a disorder that makes a person feel excessive uneasiness, often leading to panic attacks

automatic Done without thought or intention

chaotic A state of confusion and disorder

coping mechanism Coping skills or behavioral tools that people use to relieve stress or ease pain

depression A disorder that makes a person feel low, tired, and sometimes that things are hopeless

disorder A medical condition

dissociated Disconnected or separate

forums A format or place where ideas and views can be exchanged

gender Sexual identity; males or females, each considered as a group

inflicting To cause something unpleasant to be suffered by someone

psychologists People who study the human mind, emotions, and behavior

recovery A return to a normal, healthy state or mood

recurring To happen again, or a thought, image, or memory that repeatedly comes back to a person's mind

regret To feel sorry, disappointed, or distressed about

self-esteem How a person thinks about themselves and their own worth

therapy Treatment designed to relieve or heal a disorder

treatment Medical care given to someone with an illness or disorder

Index